More Praise for *Santa Ana*

In these constantly shifting, rest an urban landscape mostly seen through the eyes of a brilliant, sometimes homeless, often nearly unhinged speaker. Populated by coyotes, threatened by wildfires, Swensen's Southern California is a place where everything seems to speak at once, where characters teeter on the verge of violence and the Santa Ana winds "run through the fields with a jacaranda of fire tucked behind their ear." These are electric, harrowing poems.

~ Kevin Prufer

Auden tell us that a poet should have not just an internal censor but a censorate, one made up of "a sensitive only child, a practical housewife, a logician, a monk, an irreverent buffoon and…a brutal, foul-mouthed drill sergeant who considers all poetry rubbish." In Russel Swensen's poetry, he lets these and a whole host of others have their say, and the sense you get is that after listening very carefully, and even taking their advice, he promptly gives them the middle finger. The result is a unique, uncanny sensibility, one that unites the ugliness of the world with the beautiful, the unsettling with the ordinary, the peculiar and strange with the familiar and inviting. You're going to laugh when you're not supposed to, and you're going to feel affinities to people whose lives you might otherwise pity or shrink away from. "You're clever and you have élan," Swensen writes, which is how you'll feel reading these poems. "But you can't shake the feeling," which is how you're going to feel long after.

~ Hayan Charara

Russel Swensen

SANTA ANA

Black Lawrence Press

Black Lawrence Press
www.blacklawrence.com

Executive Editor: Diane Goettel
Book Design: Rebecca Maslen
Cover photo: Elizabeth Hall

ISBN: 978-1-937854-22-5

Published 2012 by Black Lawrence Press, an imprint of Dzanc Books *for Liz*

Here's how it happens. You're at the trailhead in Elysian Park and a man on an ATV drives up and hops off. He tells you there are coyotes ahead and that they outnumber you seven to one. He says you have no chance. He says they outnumber your dog seven to one. And you're confused because you're in the middle of the park and unsure in which direction the coyotes have been seen. Have they slunk out behind you or are they waiting up ahead? You try to ask the man on the ATV but he just laughs and drives off. Now you're not sure if he was serious. But there are coyotes in these hills. You've seen them in the moonlight gliding forward as though on wheels. You want to say I've seen them too but the man is now a speck in the distance. This is Los Angeles and maybe he just meant there are coyotes and they do on average outnumber you and your tiny rat terrier and her strawberry spots. Or maybe he meant coyotes in a larger sense that there are predatory things in the hills filming spots for all terrain vehicles or throwing wrap parties in Beverly Hills (laughing softly and stopping when you walk into the room). Or maybe he just meant that you have no chance whatsoever that he saw something in your hesitant step that looked cowed and overwhelmed. Don't discount this possibility. Everything she said last night can be seen in the middle of you like a single mourner in the village square. Or it's just a joke and he wants to scare you. Why would coyotes be out in the daylight? Don't they evaporate in the sun, don't they run when they hear pebbles stirring in the ground? It doesn't help that you're hungover and sore and that everything is quivering as though touched with a faint breeze. Troubled into being. This isn't a good part of your decision making process. You think you could probably kill a coyote with your canteen. You should have brought a canteen. If they come at you how do you make sure your dog is safe while you vanquish them? You need someone else to hold her then you can beat the coyotes against flat rocks or throw them off the path watch them roll through the brush like bowling balls— you will laugh heartily. But then you'll look up and your dog will be missing. You know this with a terrible sense of certainty. You'll look up and call her name.

The sky spread with a knife.

All day, the ash settled slowly over the deer paths. The sky was red and rust and the pussy willows, if there were pussy willows, wept.

She had a tattoo of a star on one shoulder; she had scars and smelled like lilac. In the tub her bones moved like veins.

He was a drifter from Koreatown, loved that Karaoke, dessert at the H.M.S. Bounty: the pit of an apricot adrift in a saucer of honey.

Standing at the door as if made of brass; his hands came together like cymbals. Possibly at the Brass Monkey or underwater.

Where she saw him first. As he lost his job, if he had a job. He stopped, clasping his hands together as in prayer, the moment he saw her.

Or she shook the ash from her hair like dew and his hands remained outstretched, long after the dazzle of her scent.

She said yes; they walked through the lallating light. The
question was the question, avoiding representation.

You're a tour guide. The room you've been subletting is being shown along with the rest of the house to a bevy of interested parties. There are girls from New Zealand and Sweden. There's a faint pattern of condensation on your cheeks. There's a Psychology professor from UCLA. Several twenty somethings with no readily identifiable source of income. Their phones have video capabilities. Someone at a great remove looks through the screen, someone ushers the phone through the room. It's strange to watch someone describe a place to a thing. You expect subtitles you were promised subtitles. But instead a rootless confusion, a broken comb. Why do these people have to be so selfish? You're not sure why exactly but every time someone fingers the fixtures you feel a little bit dirty. The gesture seems private and at this point they're still your fixtures. That's all. And if people keep playing with them water will come flooding out. It'll pour out your forehead and your fingertips and it will smell bitter and acrid. It will be like urine that is dark as tea. You don't want to cry dark urine tea. They're the ones who keep touching things. They're going to make you spill and this makes you anxious which makes you feel like water is definitely welling up and becoming inevitable. Nervousness distends your stomach. You're like a plague baby in aviation shades. Shifting your weight constantly from one foot to the other. Even though you know the effort is doomed. They want to make sure things work. You don't have a job. That's part of the problem right there. They have jobs and girlfriends and you have water. They want to check each and every faucet. You're looking too long at the drains. You're making people uncomfortable. You smile wanly. It makes people uncomfortable. You walk into the walk-in closet and hope it passes. You describe the closet but tell them they can't come in. You're shouting but remain calm. You're not shouting anything unreasonable. You describe dimension and utility. The shoe racks for instance. The feeling of imminence isn't entirely asexual. When it happens. Does it have to happen? You don't want to have to explain to people that you're not a spigot. They'll probably give you a long look. Your shoes are filling up with blood. There's no way of telling that it's blood. Someone has to take your shoes off and check.

If you've never had a home.

He puts her under water, she stays under water. Her veins move like eels, like black reels of forgotten film.

In the stills, she stands askew as if the floor were slanted or her skirt slipping, the ledge of her hips falling out of frame.

Clouds of flour harden on their skin; occasionally they open an oven, looking inside for a lost child.

First the edges brown to the air, then blackness at the center, then it's a flower, then you have to drop the picture.

You could say the camera wavers. You could say that.

He asks her to be like a bonsai, she knots her limbs in front of the sliding glass door, one foot in the spilled earth.

Toed in with animal grace or *alive to possibility.*

There's a certain kind of poetry, a certain kind of life, that's like tracing your finger in a swift running brook.

But this isn't it.

The hermit crab, for instance.

Moves from one abandoned house to the next, wears each as raiment, one day you find him standing in your living room with only his eyes visible.

Or the plated glass where his eyes should be.

And he is screaming that you have forgotten him. He is screaming, this stranger in the abandoned home.

His forearm unravels on the ash-scuffed rug. How wet, how terrible, *but why*, the boy says, *would you ever bother cleaning up?*

Genuinely confused. The stranger is your friend for some time, several days, possibly weeks. Steals your favorite blouse.

You find a condom in the dirt just outside the house.

You stare into the sun until black dots begin to bubble up, as if from within it, until black dots, clustered like grapes, are all you see.

Each of them saying *listen, listen, please listen*. You have to listen to me.

Please.

You weren't always such a lousy tour guide. At first you described the home with genuine affection. You pointed out the fig trees and the blood oranges. You made some sort of apology for the mangos "I know they *look* impoverished, but..." You pointed out that the sunroom could easily be converted to a studio. That the driveway went from the front of the property all the way back to the landlord's house. "You could use it as a landing strip," you were telling people and they laughed uneasily because you were trying too hard. That's ok. You're getting fifty dollars for doing this and it's probably a good thing if your efforts are visible. You feel like "effort" is written on your forehead in shiny black magic marker. You felt like that, once. But something's changed. Now you describe the house as "endless despair, like a valley" the porch with its sofa where you used to smoke "freeing but kind of scary at the same time like when you really like this here cloud and then you see it on a horse but then the horse runs away." You're getting some looks at this point. But you look back and take off your glasses you want them to know you you're serious. You stare very intently and ask pointed questions about commute. You weigh in on the local Thai and make sure to mention the proximity of the park. You discuss the relative merits of the two closest libraries. You are nothing if not assiduous and diligent. But something turns. There's just too many of them. It's seven to one every time and you don't really want to leave. These people hate you and that's why you have to leave.

Paul confronts you. He wants to know why you've been saying such terrible things. You tell him you can't understand him because of the wheelchair. You say that it's like going through a tunnel. He runs his hand over his bald head as though checking it for scratches. There are a few. He doesn't own any cats so you have to wonder. But you didn't mean to wonder out loud. Just lately things come out of you all sorts of things. You've lost your filter. There are all these hairy black flies inside of you and when they come out they sound cruel. They didn't use to come out. Now you're a pretty lousy window and you're still talking and Paul tells you to "cut the crap." He's not a bad guy even if he has things and you don't. There's a shawl in his lap though it's not unseasonably cold. You're really not sure why you're so attached to your newfound malice. Or why you briefly envision strangling Paul to death with the garden hose. You're afraid that he can see you imagining it and that he won't know that you're joking. You try to put your hand on his shoulder in a reassuring fashion but he doesn't find it reassuring at all. You offer to water the plants. The plants express no opinion as to whether they think this is a good idea or not. Paul asks you to stop crying. But you're not crying.

You wake up shaky and unsure. What city what time zone what bus; why did you fall asleep with your face pressed against the glass. Now your cheek feels sticky and dark. Outside the window you see an oil derrick in the backyard of a craftsman house. You pick up your phone but you keep dropping it. You can't feel your hands. It's hard to type when you're suffering from the delusion that you have no hands. The city used to soothe you. But you took it too many times. You've developed quite the tolerance.

Imagine the eye is a dandelion, for a long time, you're very careful with it, and then there's a knock at the door.

Delicately spraying out and carried by the wind. *Oh*, the oak trees moan, *not him again. We all know what the means* said the fireplace.

Who's there, someone's there, says the stairs. With the exact intonation of a teacher shouting *head's up, seven up.*

Remember, says the boy, *it doesn't matter who. Remember*, he says pressing his nails into her palm until they wet.

Remember, they're not real. Rushing out the back door, half-dressed, she stumbles & falls into a deep, deep sleep.

A memory, actually, filling her head entirely, as helium fills a balloon, as they stumble through the flowerbeds next door, she remembers.

She remembers a fire escape in winter, the railing crustacean with rust. The sun and the afternoon and she was nineteen.

A boy with greyhound skin gave her a cigarette. *It's the last one* he told her. *It's the last one ever.* And if there was snow, it emphasized the point.

There was snow.

Everything delicate with ice and turning white then, as the evening came, a luminous blue, aurora New York, until a final darkness.

That fell over each building and each fire escape, until there was no other left, but the one they sat upon.

What are you thinking, he says. *What are you always thinking?*

The beginnings of the fires are a mystery to almost everyone that wasn't directly involved (but they're not a mystery to you). Some say they're an answer to the girl's body, she's the chum thicking the waters here. Some speculate about the fire ecology of Los Angeles and its indigenous plant life. The way in which it is actually built to burn and replace itself. And some say that the urban planners of the city proper imitated this model in almost exacting fashion. Or the canyons. There's always something bedraggled and bloody in the canyons (recording songs). Making the occasional trip down for provisions. Lots of people say when the first spark is found it will be in the fist of an angry black populace. But they don't say it that seriously. It's just one of the jokes making the rounds that year. Girls shivering in the booths at the Cha Cha lounge: "someone just looked over my profile pic at Central Casting." All alone on Mulholland. "Someone just clicked me on OkCupid." "My high school drug dealer just folded his clothes neatly on top of his bed, looked sadly out the window." Of course the obvious suspect is the wind. The wind, in the foothills, with a head full of mescaline. The Santa Ana winds which you had to have explained to you when you first came here (several distinct fashions ago). Your good friend the internet said: "Gastrointestinal effects such as hypermotility and psychological effects such as anxiety and irritability can be produced by these winds. They are dry offshore winds often responsible for the spread of wild fire in the Los Angeles area. These effects are thought to be produced by increased levels of serotonin in the body." Your other friend, Wendy, with her nitid fingers defrocking a Dixie beer (whispering): "it makes you feel like your brain is chewing on itself." You yourself have definitely felt enraged by bus drivers and have said some despicable things to women. A plain dish looks dirty in the right light. And since you know categorically what started these particular fires in the year of our Lord 2008 and why they can't be contained, you're not going to deny that the winds themselves have been a great help. They are like loud music playing adjacent to an argument only just become a domestic dispute. You implore them to stop and turn back to the woman but the music gets louder and you threaten it. And your woman tries to leave the room and by now you've just about had it with this shit, you know? The imperative thing to know about the

Santa Ana winds is that they play along. That they run through the fields with a jacaranda of fire tucked behind their ear. They sit merrily in the back of the squad car. They won't say a word.

Difficult btw to pinpoint exactly when you made the transition from "abode challenged" to out and out homeless. The distinction's a fine one. Was it when your place was leased to the nice Libyan couple who brewed their own beer? It could not have been then. For you tucked your rat terrier Zulu in your arms and drove off. There was much waving. You had a car. You had a dog. You didn't stop to think that you weren't going anywhere for quite some time. But you did arrive somewhere (several times). Couches were offered to you. You nestled against the blue flank of an air mattress and understood gratitude. There were interviews and you were blank as a page. But nothing came of them (except for the wind that was turning around and around in your head like a dog before it sleeps) and you were nudged to other, less plush but still highly serviceable couches. You slept on floors with and without comforters. There were ceiling tiles and linoleum like love is just some big elaborate hoax. It was when the dog. "And your little dog too." But you can't dwell on that now.

Are you for real? she asked you the first time you met her. You were at the Brass Monkey one thing led to another, the sky cut up, something sharp (write it). You assured her that you were. But you felt a moment of doubt. You look in the mirror and you can't tell if the shirt suits you. Or is for sure a shirt. A feeling like that: anxiety without conviction though very much present in the back of your mind: a something with teeth. You went into that whatever light with her. But in your mind the wind was puzzled and turned over card after card in an attempt to read further into this question. "We're not sure," is what the wind finally came back with. "We'll keep looking," and never heard from again, sneaking around—the wind rustles the pages of her little notebook all you have or all you have now. Look at the pages she says while you lie in painted darkness. They're flipping they're flipping out.

Does it mean having things that buzz inside you and a stick out handle?

Or *how could you think at a time like this*, running his hands down her tawny length (*your body*, he tells her, *is made of rope*).

Or as they run, "*you there,*" "*stop,*" "*wait,*" or even the jacarandas are screaming *you need to help us you never ever help us.*

She doesn't know how to help a flower. Or how to explain that they need help. He goes into town, or east of La Brea, for supplies.

She's always in a gas station bathroom, staring at the mirror. She combs her hair, the soot comes out in mossy strands.

She's afraid to come out, of course. Because then she'll know which gas station she's in. She'll have to do something next.

They stay just ahead of the flames, she claims the red bull is chasing them out to sea, his fiery hooves erasing the cigarette butts they leave behind them.

He props himself up on one elbow and says *Listen, I need to know, Are you awake? Listen. Are you in control? Are you listening?*

The moonlight shattered by the dark, rustling leaves outside the window.

Shattered by dark leaves into countless white spiders that move silently across her calm, expressionless face.

White spiders pour across her navel and the sheets with the wine-red stain that resembles an elephant without a trunk.

She knows they're not real.

Is this the fifth house, the sixth? How many times have you moved from abandoned home to abandoned home? You really don't know. But the morning seems hard and grating. The air feels like paper against your skin. It makes you sick. You roll over but she's not there. The faintest smell of lavender clings to the sheets. It's not her scent. But it's what you have to work with so you linger in it for a moment before springing to your feet and rummaging through the house as though it were a cleverly wrapped package with something really *neat* hidden in its folds and wrapping. On the bureau, a note, a real see-you-later you're thinking. Some real greeting card shit and at this point too? But it's her crabbed mandarin script. That is somehow like a broken hand lit up on an x-ray. That is somehow all you want right now. All you want to do is take it home and lie with it over you like mosquito netting. If only you could control what it says. If only you could stop the web's tightening grasp.

The wind, which has been at their back, which has ushered their enemies from their homes and into dark sedans and eastern caravans, finds them. Finds them out.

Hollow in their wicker chairs.

Slumped over nowhere in Pomona. With his skin like stained glass. With his mind an aria of blinding light.

Beached on the patio with aluminum turning white. Dug up.

Or undermined.

Second star to the right, he murmurs, touching one shoulder then the other, with a reverence that unnerves her.

Sylvester with the magic pebble under his tongue. The professor, in the study, with the lead pipe. And collection of jade figurines.

The girl, in the house, with the medicine cabinet.

The wind fills their heads with embers, each word stirs them, tiny sounds cause them to spark and flicker.

Her breath smells like a campfire.

I don't like it when you do that, she says.

Someone else's toothbrush, pretty much an acquired taste.
Someone else's romper. Someone else's life.

When he's asleep, black bees pour out of the faucets. Smoke signals instead of text messaging.

Do you want to play sleeping beauty do you want to play slow flames runs over the house like crimson ivy.

He throws everything she owns (which isn't much) out the window, the scraps fluttering in the rose bushes.

Follow your spirit animal out of town, the boy says.

Does it hurt, asks the Rabbit?

This fist full of soot.

This triangle in my mind.

When you are Real you don't mind being hurt.

She sits on a singed billiard table, singing *if you put your ear to an ash tray, you can hear the sea of flame replacing me.*

She says it to the boy. She says it to the wind, to the bartender at the Malibu Inn, who talks only out of the side of his mouth.

When the dog barks, when the bee stings...

Sounding, surprisingly, like hyacinths and twisted metal. On Sunset Blvd, which is to say, scarlet fever. Fear death by therapist.

He dreams they're walking through an ancient forest. The forest is her. He can't find her and it grows dark.

When he wakes up, shaking, she whispers to him, *the boys in this city make the coyotes look temperate.*

She paints her nails white.

She says

when they take me apart, they will find a tunnel.

You lean over the bureau like a surgeon over a basin. How you rinse your hands in its possibilities. How tremulous you are, how delicate, the truth is you've yet to stick a finger in, the basin's water a thin dark skim. And when you take the note in your hands the paper feels like butter, cold, nearly frozen butter.

Zool. The name, in Mexico and now in the United States (hurray!), of the prairie— or barking-wolf (*Canis latrans*) of the Pacific slope of North America. *Cayeute*. A *coyote*, is a mammal of the order *carnivore*. On Christmas a mammal of the order *carnivore,* unwrapped some oil stained rags on my porch like it was bringing me a present. The oil stained rags were part of my cat. They seemed like maybe they had been an important part. "This is what you get for living in California." I think my mother actually said that. She was an awful woman. It was awful. I thought a mistake had been made. Her head was a bloody mess. I think it was her head. My cat's head. My mom's head was fine although quite bald. Coyotes smuggle people across the border. Everyone knows that. They wear fancy driving gloves and act real anxious, you don't even need the subtitles. You know the story here. Somehow they're always caught on film. Like coyotes are maybe not that bright though their eyes do that thing you know? Where they've caught the headlights and the headlights are in their eyes and they can't get out and you have to look. I mean, you could look away but you don't. Let's see. "Coyotes are sad" is what I was thinking when I woke up. That's why I'm writing this down. Because it seemed like a really weird thing to think. Like, they've got so much to be sad about, you know? Licking their little paws in the dumpster behind the drive-thru. Voting in their little councils with their tiny dark bones. Holding thimbles full of clear liquor, never spilling a drop. Coyotes are dainty. Coyotes are noble. But maybe they are sad ok how are they sad? A coyote keeps his sadness in the glove-box. A coyotes sits in the front seat it has the head of a coyote. The sadness of the coyote is a napkin with something dark seeping through it. El Coyote is in West Hollywood. I can't believe I ever lived there. Not that "right here right now" is exactly the sort of thing to write home about. You know, all I really think about these days is Wile E. Coyote. Throwing himself into ravines and falling into trenches. Poor Wile E and trying so hard and with everyone watching. Like a meeting where they ask for your ideas and then laugh at you behind your back. That's what his life's like. And another thing I can't get out of my head (out of my head, out of my head) is this here *folk singer*, right? Who was hiking up in Canada and the coyotes tore her apart. This Taylor Mitchell chick. And this wildlife biologist, this expert, right? Was on TV saying it was because they thought she was a *deer*. Like, I guess you can be too graceful. I guess you can be too graceful! And last night I think I was the girl again, I was wearing a wrangler shirt, I said *my pearl snaps are having a nervous fucking breakdown.* And the sky spreading its legs. For another big star. In California which is everywhere. And this other girl Ashley who held her head up high like she was afraid it was going to fall off. And my dad in front of the tv with his guts on the tray eating it all up and his licorice black lips wrinkling his wet nose the smell was the only thing that bothered him. And— you can't read anymore. You crumple the note up and it falls into the wastebasket slow as the seed of a whirlybird. You're clever and you have élan. But you can't shake the feeling.

What has happened?

Say something, he says. *Say something,* says the wind, and laughs, running its hand over the jagged edges of the window glass.

Something, she says and turns away.

You're impossible, he says. *There's no talking to you.*

How stiff they are, how unwelcome, when not an hour ago they passed the same breath back and forth, stoned, and soft.

But that was long ago. And her tear, which just fell, holds the entire room reflected in a crystal speck.

Their silhouettes revolve within the tear like oil in water. Their reflections circle each other like boxers.

But the tear is a real tear, a pearl tear, shimmering in the turtle-faced ash tray they'd found on the porch.

The turtle-faced ash tray withered with cigarettes.

Still-lit cigarettes writhe, as though uncomfortable. The cigarettes squirm. One of them says, *please, sir can I have some water?*

Another, nearly nub, explains that it does not mind burning, only the time that it takes. Its voice a dry-wired rasp.

The boy hears the cigarettes. The girl hears the cigarettes. She says, *please sir, can I have some more,* her laughter is an ugly thing.

The aquarium sings a sad song without any words.

Of course they were pink— the sort of pink you feel bad about.

She is made of mink and sugar and good clean water. She is made of long silences and falling leaves that turn opal upon the lawn.

You could have washed your face in her.

But you didn't.

He has a machine inside him. Something awful. A blood tractor. Something with belts and gauges and feeding ramps.

She knows.

I shouldn't have said that, says the girl.

I'm sorry, he says. *Me too*, she says.

It's the wind, he says. *It's the wind she* says, and the moon lies limp across the charred horizon, like a white-gloved hand.

How terrible it is when things work out. How easily you are fooled into thinking you've discovered something about the world a way of navigating through its crags and thickets that others have somehow never discovered. How you marvel at the goodness of the world.

In the springtime, it is not unusual to see a coyote wearing a jacaranda behind his ear. By which I mean, a small purple hole where the bullet went in. In the world of Peter S. Beagle, the surf is full of unicorns, bellowing in pain. In a similar way, the Santa Ana winds are full of coyotes. Can't you feel them? Running around in your head and tearing at the haunches tearing at the brain. Every word leaves a tooth in the mind.

Seems to me like you need to decide what it is you really want to know. Is it why I left him or is it why I stayed with him as long as I did? Do you want to know where it all went wrong? Would you like to see the birthmark on my shoulder? Would you like the penny from beneath my tongue, the face worn smooth from all the talk. All the words, all the big ones, all the ones that really had it coming. Do you want to know what "really" happened? Do you want to hear how it all began? The sky was spread with a knife. Are you wondering how I ended up here, in the Tiki Ti, drinking a Blood & Sand? Do you want to know why the crowd chants or what it is they're chanting (I know, you can't quite make it out). Once upon a time, there was a boy who met a girl and he put the burning city in her hair. Are you scientifically curious as to the extent matches played in our lovemaking or, when we played shadow puppets, which animal we chose and which animal ate the other first. Is this one of those "I just want to know what you're *really* like" sort of things. Is this your way of saying you want to play lost and found. Do you think maybe this is the beginning of a new story and you its star? Is that thing on your face what I think it is? Has the radiation sickness kicked in. Listen, I'm not fucking with you. I understand the situation. You bought me a drink and I nodded like a bobblehead doll (my head lolling as though on the verge of falling off, my shoulders in this light). I agreed. That you could buy me the drink you'd bought me and that I would tell you one thing. One true thing. That I would not make up stories. That I would stop making up stories. That I would fall silent for a moment and look, really look, within myself, before telling you something real. Something as awful as a last name or a date of birth, something uncomfortable. Because that's what we all want. We want to be trusted with the lowest part. And that's fine. That's fine. I have questions too. I want to know which childhood was truly tragic (piano wire and grease burns), who the good guy is, why kissing made him so uncomfortable, scared even, did I find it exhilarating. I want to know what it would be like to touch someone, really touch someone, without meaning to. But I'm tired. I think if someone told me, if they told me anything, one single thing, I'd scream. Did you ever hear about the wild parrots of Pasadena? They look like metal and OZ and seem too large for any single branch, they're fat on blossoms and resentment. They look like they were baked, not born. Except you never really see them, you just remember seeing them. But you hear them. You hear them singing, even in the dark. They're refugees. Like me, I guess, like me, they escaped from a pet store some lunatic set on fire (he too, had begun to struggle to communicate, how we should read his fire, I really can't say). I was screaming in my cage, I was the cat who had lost her paws, because she was ashamed of them. I begged him to let me go but he didn't and here I am, slow churning flame, frothing flame in a borrowed dress. Funny how I always assumed he died in the fire, surrounded by birds popping like fireworks in their cages, dogs turning into violins cases of flame with dogs within them. I mean, it's funny how badly we want to believe. He probably wasn't even real. It was probably an electrical problem. But the birds survived, some of them, and they're still around. Flitting around Pasadena as if scored there, each singing their little flame song. And they are their song. Each of them a single, unbearable, searing note. And we sing along. We've been singing along all along. Gathered in our uniforms and shiny with merit badges ("Can Put A Condom On With Only Her Mouth" "Can Get Dressed in Total Darkness") around their campfire, their city, this funhouse narrative, this terrible script. The wild parrots of Pasadena, has a real ring to it, doesn't it? A real ring, the kind you see flickering at the bottom of the pool. Someone was going to give it to me or somebody did, whatever. Our lady of whatever, whatever. Amen. Whatever. You want to know about winter as a blanket, why he couldn't cry alone (he had to wake me, I had to watch), you'd love to hear about the year I dressed up as a petting zoo (look at your ragged little breath). You'd like to know about this *dress* and what's really in it. You want to know how the fires started, true, that's how it began, but now you want to know what the fires meant. Which means you're lost, I can't help you anymore. I because, I mean, you don't know how to listen. I keep telling you. I've been telling you always. I'm at the top of the stairs watching them leave and I'm telling them and I'm telling myself to be brave and as for him and me and the lepidopteral summer of flames which began I keep telling you and telling you it began to and telling you and telling you what happened was

ACKNOWLEDGEMENTS

The author would like to volunteer that the world would suck eggs without Elizabeth Hall, Jessica Hallock, and Jessalyn Zachary Joy Wakefield. This manuscript is heavily indebted to the criticism and support of Glenn Shaheen and Hayan Charara. Early (and necessary) encouragement was also give by Matthew Olzmann, Tarfia Faizullah, and Paul Otremba. I would also like to thank my editor Diane Goettel for putting up with a Very Difficult Boy, Jessica Novak (talker-off-of-ledges) for soothing said Difficult Boy, and Danielle Dubois, for acts of useful treason. Lastly, a wine drenched thanks to Craig Arnold, without whom none of this would have been possible. The world is impoverished by his absence but blame my poetry existing on his presence.

photo by Karyna McGlynn

RUSSEL SWENSEN currently teaches at Prairie View A&M University. He earned his MFA in fiction from the California Institute of the Arts and his doctorate in poetry from the University of Houston. His work has appeared in *Black Clock, Quarterly West, Prick of the Spindle, FRiGG, The Collagist*, and elsewhere.